LIVING IN HARD TIMES

by Gary Miller

★ Strategy Focus

Before you read, look at the photographs.
Predict what you will learn about children
who lived during the Great Depression.

HOUGHTON MIFFLIN   BOSTON

Key Vocabulary

cheap inexpensive

depot railroad station

determination strong intention to achieve a goal

provisions necessary supplies, especially food

urgency the need to do something quickly

wares items for sale

Word Teaser

What kind of **wares** might you wear?

It was the summer of 1931. A group of teenagers stood in a city railroad yard. They couldn't get on the train at the depot, like the other passengers. They had no money to buy tickets.

Instead, they hid in the bushes by the track. When a train passed, they jumped onto a boxcar.

The teens could have been seriously hurt. But they were willing to take that chance. They were filled with a sense of urgency. Riding the rails was their only hope. Maybe they could find work somewhere else, far away from their homes and families.

In the 1930s, Americans everywhere suffered through a difficult time. Businesses closed down. Millions of people lost their jobs. Hundreds of thousands of young Americans traveled by rail to search for work. This period was called the Great Depression.

The Great Depression changed the lives of most young Americans. Families struggled to buy provisions. Many people went hungry. In cities, people waited in long lines to get free food. Some children moved in with relatives to save money.

Children who lived in the countryside worked on farms, helped raise animals, and tended gardens for food. They hunted wild animals for meat. Some families took eggs, milk, and other products to the town store. They traded these items for other wares.

Life was hardest for people in the part of the country known as the Dust Bowl, which covered parts of six states. The area was rich in farmlands. But in 1931, a drought started in this area. For eight years, farms got very little rain. Dry winds carried huge clouds of soil into the air. Black dust fell everywhere. It choked out crops. It destroyed farm machinery.

The Dust Bowl

People struggled to keep dust out of their homes. Children even wore masks when they walked to school. But nothing could stop the dust.

After years of misery, people began to leave the Dust Bowl. Many families moved to California to look for work. But there were not enough jobs there either. Many families ended up in temporary camps. They made their homes in shacks and tents.

Times were hard for everyone. But people stuck together. They helped each other. They were filled with determination to survive.

People looked for inexpensive ways to forget their troubles. Radio provided cheap entertainment for families with electricity. But many rural areas did not yet have electricity. So people on farms gathered to play games and sing their own music. Children played baseball and a game called "kick the can."

In 1932, Americans elected a new president. Franklin D. Roosevelt wanted to make life better for Americans. So did his wife, Eleanor Roosevelt.

Franklin Roosevelt started programs to create jobs. The government hired people to build bridges, plant trees, and even write books. These new jobs didn't pay much. But they gave people a feeling of pride. For some, life slowly improved.

Franklin D. Roosevelt ▼

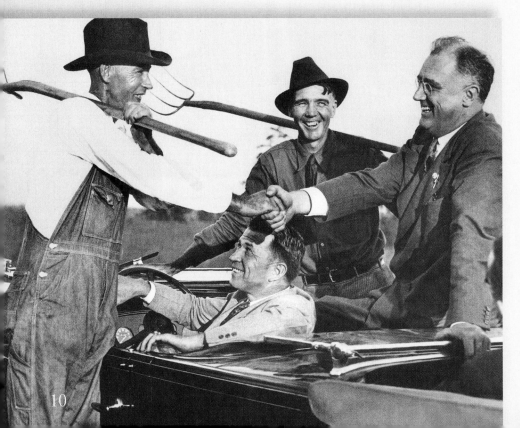

Eleanor Roosevelt reached out to the children of the Great Depression. Many children wrote letters asking for her help. They asked for coats for warmth, and shoes and clothes to wear to school.

Mrs. Roosevelt received more than 30,000 letters during her first year in the White House. She couldn't reply to all the children who contacted her, of course. Instead, she started government programs to help them and other children like them.

▼ **Eleanor Roosevelt**

In 1939, World War II began. Millions of Americans found work building weapons and other materials. People started to earn money again. The Depression was over.

No one who lived through that period would ever forget it, though.

Putting Words to Work

1. Why did people seek **cheap provisions** during the Depression?

2. Complete the following sentence:
   When I saw my dog, I was filled with a sense of **urgency** because _____.

3. Describe a time you acted with **determination** to reach a goal.

4. What might you find at a **depot**?

5. **PARTNER ACTIVITY:** Think of a word you learned in the text. Explain its meaning to your partner and give an example.

Answer to Word Teaser
clothing